For Olivia

Henry Holt and Company, *Publishers since 1866*
Henry Holt® is a registered trademark of Macmillan Publishing Group, LLC
175 Fifth Avenue, New York, NY 10010 • mackids.com

Library of Congress Control Number: 2018936458
ISBN 978-1-250-18593-8

Our books may be purchased in bulk for promotional, educational, or business
use. Please contact your local bookseller or the Macmillan Corporate
and Premium Sales Department at (800) 221-7945 ext. 5442 or by
e-mail at MacmillanSpecialMarkets@macmillan.com.

First edition, 2018 / Designed by April Ward
Printed in China by RR Donnelley Asia Printing Solutions Ltd.,
Dongguan City, Guangdong Province

1 3 5 7 9 10 8 6 4 2

ROBOT IN LOVE

T. L. McBETH

GODWIN BOOKS

Henry Holt and Company ♦ New York

It was a day
like any other.

Then I saw her.

I had never seen anyone so beautiful.

She was so shiny.

I wanted to say something,
but I was too shy.

I thought about her all day.

WOOSH!

SPLASH!

Z
Z
Z

ZAP!

I'M OK!

SIZZLE   SIZZLE

The next morning, I went back to see
if she was still there. She was!

I tried to think of something clever to say,
but I was too nervous.

My vision programming malfunctioned.

My hydraulic limbs felt weak.

My circuit board nearly jumped out of my chest unit. I would have to try again tomorrow.

The next day, I went
to our meeting spot.
I finally worked up the
courage to talk to her.

"Greetings," I said.

I looked everywhere.

NOT UNDER THIS CANINE

I was about
to give up . . .

I raced back to our meeting spot.
This time I went inside.

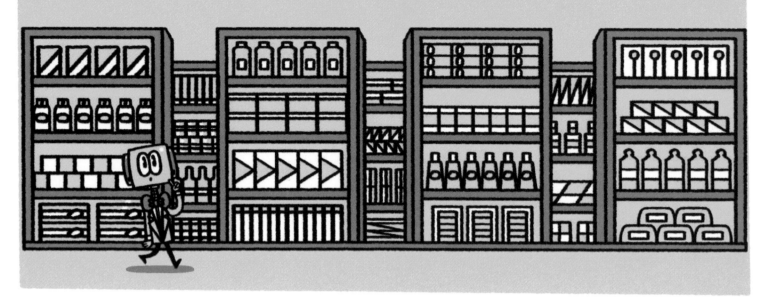

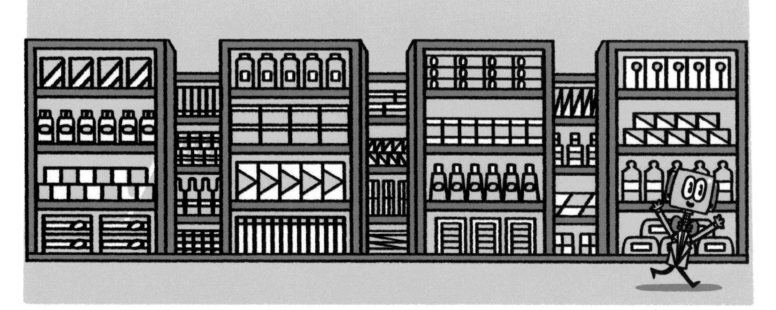

She said nothing.
But she didn't have to.

We have so much in common.

We're both shy.

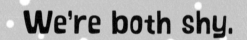

IS THAT A TOASTER?

And we both love toast.